Disney

The Never Girls

far from shore

Written by
Kiki Thorpe

Illustrated by
Jana Christy

A STEPPING STONE BOOK™
RANDOM HOUSE 🏠 NEW YORK

For Anna
—K.T.

For Mom, Lola, and Sophia, with all my love
—J.C.

Library of Congress Cataloging-in-Publication Data
Thorpe, Kiki.
Far from shore / written by Kiki Thorpe ; illustrated by Jana Christy.
pages cm. — (The Never girls ; 8)
"A Stepping Stone book."
Summary: "The Never Girls have heard about a boy who lives in Never Land—
a legendary boy who brings adventure wherever he goes. A boy named Peter Pan.
Kate can't wait to meet him. But Tinker Bell knows that Peter is also good at causing
trouble. Will this be an adventure, or a disaster?"— Provided by publisher.
ISBN 978-0-7364-3302-0 (paperback) — ISBN 978-0-7364-8166-3 (lib. bdg.) —
ISBN 978-0-7364-3303-7 (ebook)
[1. Fairies—Fiction. 2. Magic—Fiction. 3. Characters in literature—Fiction.
4. Adventure and adventurers—Fiction.] I. Christy, Jana, illustrator.
II. Disney Enterprises (1996–) III. Title.
PZ7.T3974Far 2015
[Fic]—dc23
2014023980

randomhousekids.com/disney
Printed in the United States of America
10 9 8 7 6 5 4 3 2 1

This book has been officially leveled by using the F&P Text Level Gradient™ Leveling System.

Never Land

Far away from the world we know, on the distant seas of dreams, lies an island called Never Land. It is a place full of magic, where mermaids sing, fairies play, and children never grow up. Adventures happen every day, and anything is possible.

There are two ways to reach Never Land. One is to find the island yourself. The other is for it to find you. Finding Never Land on your own takes a lot of luck and a pinch of fairy dust. Even then, you will only find the island if it wants to be found.

Every once in a while, Never Land drifts close to our world . . . so close a fairy's laugh slips through. And every once in an even longer while, Never Land opens its doors to a special few. Believing in magic and fairies from the bottom of your heart can make the extraordinary happen. If you suddenly hear tiny bells or feel a sea breeze where there is no sea, pay careful attention. Never Land may be close by. You could find yourself there in the blink of an eye.

One day, four special girls came to Never Land in just this way. This is their story.

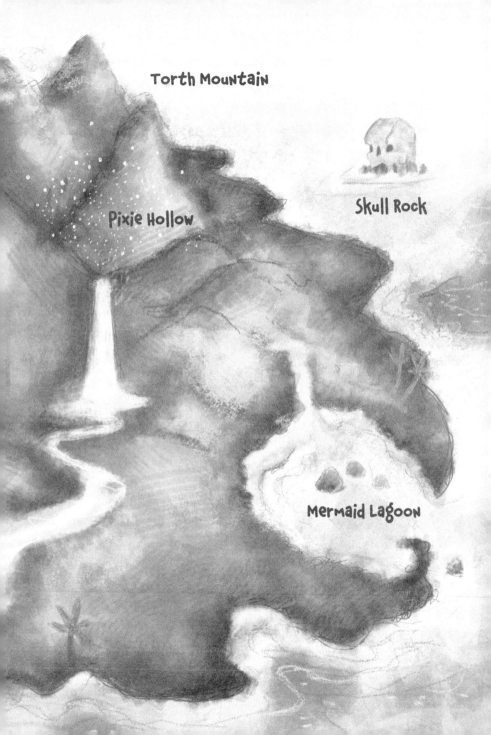

chapter 1

Kate McCrady lay on her back in the meadow. Above her, framed by wild-flowers, was the bright blue sky of Never Land. Now and then, a fairy flew past carrying an armful of bluebells or a fat chestnut. But the fairies never looked down or seemed to notice the tall, red-headed girl hiding in the grass.

Kate held perfectly still, even when a grasshopper jumped onto her arm. She stared up patiently at the blue sky, waiting . . . waiting . . .

Nearby, the grass rustled. Someone was coming.

"Where did Kate go?" Kate recognized the voice of her best friend, Mia Vasquez.

"I don't know. I thought I saw her here a minute ago." That was Kate's other best friend, Lainey Winters.

"Guys, wait for me!" called a third girl. It was Mia's little sister, Gabby.

They were getting closer. Kate stifled a giggle.

When they were almost on top of her, Kate popped up from the grass, shouting, "BOO!"

The girls shrieked. The flowers in their arms went flying.

Kate stood up, laughing. "Ha, ha! Got you!"

Mia gave her a playful shove. "Geez, Kate. You really scared me," she said. She bent to pick up the flowers she'd dropped. More flowers were woven into her long, curly hair. "You told us you were going to pick some daisies."

"I did pick daisies. They're here somewhere. . . ." Kate looked around and spotted them. The daisies were on the ground beneath her, squished. Kate shrugged. "Oh, well. I guess that means no more daisy chains for me."

"You're the one who said you wanted to try making them," Lainey pointed out.

The friends had spent the morning weaving flowers with the garden-talent fairies in Pixie Hollow. Mia, Lainey, and Gabby were all wearing colorful wreaths of buttercups, bluebells, daisies, and tea roses.

"I guess it *sounded* like more fun than it is," Kate said. Her daisy chains never came out quite right. They always looked lopsided or fell apart—even *with* the help of fairy magic.

So what, Kate thought. *There's more to life than perfect daisy chains.*

Ever since they'd discovered the secret magical passage that led from their world to Never Land, Kate and her friends visited Pixie Hollow whenever they could. Every time they went, they had a new exciting adventure.

And if it was a quiet day, like today? Well, Kate didn't mind making her own excitement.

"Listen, I was thinking we should go to the mill and ask Terence for a pinch of fairy dust. Then maybe we could go flying." Kate looked at her friends hopefully.

"No, thanks," Mia said, as Kate had feared she might. "No flying for me." When Tinker Bell had first taught the girls to fly, they'd all ended up in Havendish Stream. Since then, no matter how hard Kate tried to convince her, Mia had refused to try it again.

"Come *on*," said Kate, trying one more time. "It's just like riding a bike. You might fall a couple of times. But once you get the hang of it, it's easy!"

"Nope." Mia shook her head.

"We're in Never Land! Don't you guys want to do *anything*?" Kate asked.

"We are doing something. We're making daisy chains," Lainey said.

"I meant anything *fun*," Kate replied with a sigh.

"Why don't you go," Mia suggested.

"We can stay here and finish our flowers."

Kate didn't need to think twice. "I'll just go for a little while," she agreed. "We can meet back at the Home Tree." She could practically feel the wind on her face already!

Kate said good-bye to her friends. Then she hurried to the mill, which sat on the banks of Havendish Stream. The fairies kept their dust there, sealed up tightly in pumpkin canisters. Fairy dust was precious—it allowed the fairies to fly and do their magic.

"Going flying?" asked Terence, the dust-talent sparrow man, when he saw Kate. He sprinkled a thimbleful of dust over her.

"Just out for a spin," Kate said. She

pushed off the ground, and in a few seconds she was as high as the treetops.

Kate flew away from Pixie Hollow, toward the big bend in Havendish Stream. This was where Tinker Bell had brought them for their first flying lesson. Kate wanted to teach herself how to do a flip turn, and this was a good place to practice. The trees were spaced wide apart, and the ground was covered with soft moss.

Kate got a flying start. When she was halfway to the next tree, she tucked into a somersault, and—

"Whoops!" Kate fell out of the air. She landed on her back in the moss.

Kate sat up and glanced around, wondering if anyone had seen her fall. But she was alone. The only sound was a bird cawing in a nearby tree.

"I must not have been going fast enough," Kate said to herself. She rose into the air to try again. This time, Kate put on a burst of speed. When she reached the halfway point, she ducked into a roll—

"Oof!" Kate grunted as she landed on the ground again.

Lying on her back, Kate stared up at the branches above. Somewhere in them, the bird was cawing again.

"Cah-coo! Cah-coo!"

"Oh, be quiet," Kate grumbled as she got to her feet. This trick was turning out to be harder than she'd thought.

She tried again, flying slower. Then she tried flying faster. She tried starting the flip sooner. She tried it starting from a standstill. But each time she ended up flat on her back in the moss. And each time the bird cawed loudly, *"Cah-coo! Cah-coo!"* Kate had the feeling it was laughing at her.

She told herself she would try the flip once more before she gave up. "I'm sure I'll get it this time."

But she was shaky after so many falls. She'd barely started before she was on the ground again.

"Cah-coo-coo-coo!" the bird crowed.

Now Kate was *sure* it was laughing at her. "Buzz off!" she shouted. She snatched an acorn from the ground and hurled it into the branches.

A second later, the acorn came arcing

back through the air. It landed right at Kate's feet.

Kate stared. She was pretty sure most birds couldn't throw things—at least, not in a perfect overhand pitch. She rose and flew up into the tree. She wanted to see this bird for herself.

High among the leaves and branches, Kate looked around. Because she was looking for a bird, it took her a moment to spot him.

It wasn't a bird at all. There was a *boy* in the tree!

The boy was crouched in the crook of a branch. Kate hadn't seen him at first because he was dressed head to toe in leaves. The leaves rustled faintly as he shifted on the branch. He was so well disguised that all Kate could see of him was a pale, heart-shaped face and a few curling wisps of red hair.

The boy smiled at her. Then he pushed backward off the branch. He turned in the air, heels over head, and sped off in the opposite direction.

Kate couldn't help noticing that it was a perfect flip turn.

The boy soared away, calling back over his shoulder, *"Cah-coo! Cah-coo! Cah-coo!"*

Kate stared after him. *Who was that?*

chapter 2

Tinker Bell tightened the last bolt into place. "All right!" she called. "Let's try it again."

Tink's friend Fawn, an animal-talent fairy, was standing at the ready. She pulled a sunflower seed from her pocket and offered it to the mouse in front of her, holding it just out of his reach. "Good boy," Fawn coaxed. "Want a snack?"

The mouse scrambled after the seed. As he did, the wooden wheel he was standing on began to turn. This turned another wheel, which turned a crank that began to wind a length of rope.

"It's working!" cried the water fairy Silvermist, who was watching nearby.

They heard a zipping sound as the rope ran through a pulley at the top of a pebble well. Tink held her breath. A second later, the rope drew up a thimbleful of water from the well.

"We did it!" Tink exclaimed. "My mouse-powered water well works!"

Fawn fed the sunflower seed to the mouse, who stopped running. She and Silvermist joined Tink by the well. "Just think," Fawn said. "It only took twelve tries, three different mice, and twenty-seven sunflower seeds to get this one bucket of water."

"There were a few glitches at first," Tink admitted. "But think how much easier it will be to get water now!"

At that moment, a large shadow passed over them. The mouse looked up and started running again, frightened.

"Whoa! Stop!" cried Tink.

As the rope wound, the bucket jerked out of her hands. It swung through the air and jammed against the pulley—spilling the water over Tink's head.

As Tink wiped drops from her eyes, a pair of giant feet in sneakers landed next to the fairies. Craning her neck, Tink looked up and saw they belonged to Kate.

"Kate!" she snapped. "You can't go swooping down on fairies like that. We thought you were a hawk."

"Sorry," Kate said. She squatted down

so they could talk more easily. "Why are you all wet?"

"It's Tink's mouse-powered water well," explained Fawn. She was trying to calm down the trembling mouse.

"Apparently, it isn't Kate-proof yet," Silvermist added.

But Kate didn't seem to be listening. Her eyes were bright with excitement. "Have you seen Mia and Lainey and Gabby?" she asked the fairies. "I have something to tell them. The weirdest thing just happened—"

"Hey!" Mia said, walking up with the two other girls. "What are you talking about?"

As Kate told her friends about her trip to the forest, Tink went back to fiddling

with her invention. She tightened the
bolts, examined the wheels, and added a
bit of grease to the crank. Tink loved tinkering. She was happiest when
she had something to fix.

She was tightening a knot
in the rope when she heard
Kate say, "And when I looked
up there was a boy dressed in
leaves—"

Tink's pointy ears pricked up. "That's
Peter!" she interrupted.

"Who's Peter?" asked Kate.

"Peter Pan," said Silvermist. "He's the
Lost Boys' leader."

"I've heard of him!" Lainey said. "The
boys told me about him." On a recent
trip to Never Land, the girls had met the

Lost Boys, a group of boys who lived in Never Land's forest. "They said he was away from the island. He must have come back."

"Have you met him?" Mia asked the fairies.

The fairies nodded. "He comes to Pixie Hollow sometimes to get fairy dust so he can fly," Fawn explained.

"What's he like?" Kate asked.

"Tink could tell you," Silvermist replied. "She knows him best."

Everyone turned to look at Tink. "Oh, I don't know," she said, fiddling with the rope. "It's been a long time since I've seen him."

"But there must be something you can tell us about him," Kate said.

"Well, he's clever," Tink replied. "And brave. And he can fly as well as any fairy I know. He's funny, too. And fun to be with." She laughed, thinking about him. "Something exciting always happens when Peter's around."

"I want to meet him!" Gabby cried.

The other girls nodded. They all wanted to meet Peter. "Tink, will you take us?" Kate asked.

"Maybe that's not such a good idea," Silvermist said before Tink could answer.

"Don't be silly," Tink said. "Of course they should meet Peter. Everyone in Never Land knows him."

Fawn and Silvermist pulled Tink aside. "Are you sure about this?" Fawn whispered.

"Of course," Tink said. "It will be good

to see Peter after all this time," she added, more to herself.

"But what about the mouse-powered well?" Silvermist asked. "Don't you want to finish it?"

"I will," said Tink. "Just as soon as we're back."

Silvermist and Fawn gave each other worried looks. "You *will* come back, won't you, Tink?" Silvermist asked.

Tink knew what she meant. Years before, Tink had left Pixie Hollow to go on adventures with Peter and she hadn't returned for a long, long time.

But things are different now, Tink thought. "I promise, Silvermist," she said. "We'll just pop by to say hello. We'll be back before you know it."

Tink and the girls said good-bye to Fawn and Silvermist. Then they set out for the Lost Boys' hideout, which was deep in Never Land's forest. Tink and Kate flew, while the others walked. There was no path, so the girls made their way through slowly on foot. They climbed over tangled tree roots and pushed past giant ferns.

"Don't you wish you were flying now?" Kate said as she circled above them.

"Thanks, but no thanks," said Mia. She was inching down a steep slope. She had to hold onto leaves and branches to keep from falling. "I'm happy with both my feet on the ground— Whoops!" she cried as she lost her balance and fell. She slid down the hill on her backside and crashed into a bush.

Kate flew down and offered her a hand. Mia sighed as she pulled herself up. "Don't say it."

Kate grinned. "I didn't say a word."

"I recognize this place," Lainey said, coming up behind them. "I think we're getting close to the hideout."

Tink recognized it, too. Memories of old times with Peter came flooding back to her. There was the giant mango tree where they'd once played with a family of monkeys. And over there was Peter's favorite rock. He'd called it his study because he liked to lie there and study the clouds. None of the other boys were allowed to climb it. Tink was the only one he'd ever invited to sit there with him.

And—could it be? There was the sapling Peter had split in a dagger-throwing contest. It had grown into a tall tree. Two trees, actually. The trunks leaned against each other like a pair of friends telling secrets. Had it really been so long since she last saw Peter?

Tink wondered if he had changed. Of course, he wouldn't have grown tall like the sapling. In Never Land, children never grow up. But Tink knew someone could change in other ways—ways that couldn't always be seen.

A loud roar startled Tink from her thoughts.

The girls jumped and moved closer together.

"That sounded like a *lion*," Gabby whispered.

"It sounded *close*!" Mia said. She peered nervously at the dense forest around them. "Maybe we should go back—"

"Wait," Tink said. "Where's Kate?"

They all looked around. "She was here just a second ago," Lainey said.

The roar came again, louder. This time it was echoed by another.

"Do you think she could be in trouble?" Tink asked.

The girls glanced at each other. "Knowing Kate, I'm sure of it," Mia said.

"We have to find her," Lainey said.

"Okay. But carefully," said Tink. "We don't want to end up on the wrong side of whatever is making that sound."

The group crept forward. They hadn't gone far when they spotted Kate. She was standing with her head tipped back, looking at something up in a tree.

Mia rushed to her. "Why did you go off

like that? We have to be careful. There's something out—"

"*Shh.*" Kate cut her off. *Look,* she mouthed, pointing.

A black panther was crouched in the tree. And facing him, on the same branch, was Peter Pan.

Tink's heart gave a little leap. Her old friend looked the same as he always had—merry and full of mischief.

The panther and Peter stared each other down. The panther roared again. Peter grinned and roared back. The girls and Tink held their breath.

Suddenly, the cat sprang forward. For a moment, it seemed that Peter would hold his ground. But his foot slipped and he plummeted from the tree. The panther sprang after him.

Peter landed in the leaves and lay still. The panther sniffed him. Then, with a snort, it turned and stalked away.

chapter 3

As soon as the panther was gone, Kate
and her friends rushed to help Peter. But
as she got closer, Kate began to feel afraid.
What if he's really hurt? she thought.

The other girls seemed to have the same
fear. They'd started out running, but now
they approached him slowly. Peter lay on
his back in the leaves. His eyes were closed
and one arm was flung over his head. *He
doesn't* look *hurt,* Kate thought. If she didn't

know better, she'd have thought he was sleeping.

Tink was the only one brave enough to touch him. She brushed his cheek gently. "Peter?"

Peter's eyes popped open. "BOO!" he shouted.

The girls leaped back. Tink was so startled, her glow winked out for a full second.

Peter sprang up, grinning. He turned a somersault in the air, clearly pleased with his joke. Now the girls got their first good look at him. He was a normal-sized boy, neither very big nor very small. Aside from his leafy clothes, the most striking thing about him was his laugh. It bubbled out of him like water from a fountain. It was the kind of laugh that made you want to laugh, too.

"Peter, that was a naughty trick," Tink said.

"We thought you were dead!" Gabby exclaimed.

"Me? Never!" Peter assured her. "But now and then I have to let the panther think he's won. Otherwise, he'll get low self-confidence."

Kate could tell by his plucky grin that low self-confidence was not something Peter suffered from. "Do you fight panthers often?" she asked.

"Every Thursday," Peter replied.

Was he joking? Kate couldn't tell. But she had a strange feeling he wasn't. Peter was turning out to be even more interesting than she'd hoped. "I'm Kate," she said. "I saw you before. In the forest."

She expected him to laugh, or say, "I know." But instead, to her surprise, he bowed. "I'm Peter Pan," he said formally.

Mia, Lainey, and Gabby introduced themselves, and Peter bowed to each of them, too. Gabby giggled and curtsied back, holding the edges of her tutu. Peter

even bowed to Tink, which Kate thought was a funny way to say hello to an old friend.

But Tink just smiled and said, "It's good to see you, Peter. We came from Pixie Hollow for a visit. These girls are my friends."

"Tink's the best fairy, isn't she?" Peter said. Tink's glow turned orange. Kate had never seen her blush before.

"You've all come just in time," he said.

"In time for what?" asked Mia.

Before Peter could answer, there was a rustling nearby. Nibs and Cubby came crawling out of the hollow tree that served as the

entrance to the boys' hideout. As usual, they were dressed in their ragged animal furs. They stepped out of the tree, yawning and scratching their heads.

"Hullo. You're back," Cubby said when he saw the girls. "What did we miss?"

"Peter fought a panther in a tree!" Gabby exclaimed.

"Really?" Cubby sighed. "You never wake us up for the good stuff, Peter."

"Where are the other boys?" Lainey asked. Slightly, Tootles, and the Twins were missing.

"I sent them to the other side of the river. I planted a mango seed there, and I wanted to find out what was growing from it," Peter told her.

Mia smiled. "Wouldn't *mangos* grow from a mango seed?"

"You never know," Peter replied. "I once planted a blackberry and a whole flock of blackbirds grew."

Kate laughed. This time she was sure he was joking. Almost sure, anyway. "You were saying that we're just in time for something," she reminded him. "What are we in time for?"

"An adventure," Peter told her, which was exactly what Kate was hoping he'd say.

"What kind of adventure?" Gabby asked.

"I guess we won't know till we've had it," Peter said.

"Let's go now!" Kate said.

But Tink frowned. "We just came to say hello. We should start heading back to Pixie Hollow—"

"But then you'll miss all the fun!" Peter exclaimed.

"Oh, please let's go, Tink!" Gabby begged.

The others joined in too, pleading with Tink to come, until she grinned and threw up her hands. "All right. But just one adventure," she said, and everyone cheered.

Peter rose into the air. Kate, Nibs, and Cubby followed him. Kate was so excited she forgot her friends couldn't fly, until she heard Mia shout, "Wait!"

Kate turned. Mia, Lainey, and Gabby were running on the ground after them.

"Why don't you fly?" Peter asked them.

Two bursts of red appeared on Mia's cheeks. Kate knew Mia didn't want to admit she was afraid of flying.

"It's because they don't have any fairy dust," Kate said. Mia gave her a grateful look.

"Well, that's nothing. I'll share mine." And in a moment, Peter had blown fairy dust from his hand over each of the girls.

At once, Gabby and Lainey rose into the air. But Mia didn't move. Kate knew it was because she was thinking about falling. You couldn't fly when you were thinking about the ground.

Kate went to her and took her hand. "You can do it," she whispered. "I'll help."

Mia nodded, her lips pressed tight.

"Don't think about falling. Think about things that make you happy," Kate told her. "Birthday presents. Ferris wheels. The sound of an ice cream truck coming down the street . . ."

Mia closed her eyes, concentrating. "Chocolate cupcakes with pink frosting," she murmured. "A new dress. A nest with tiny blue eggs inside . . ."

They were rising into the air. The breeze tickled their faces. Mia cautiously opened one eye, then the other. "I'm doing it! I'm flying!"

Kate grinned. "Fun, right?"

"Just don't let go yet, okay?" Mia said.

"Don't worry," said Kate. "I've got you."

Lainey, Gabby, and the boys were ahead of them. Kate could see them darting around in the air.

"Can you go a little faster?" Kate asked.

"I think so," said Mia. "I'm starting to get the hang of it now."

They sped up. As they got closer, Kate saw that her friends were playing tag

in the air. Nibs was It. Peter was taunting him by flying around him in figure eights. Every time Nibs grabbed for him, Peter would slip just out of his reach.

But on the next loop, Peter dipped a bit too low. His leg brushed Nibs's hand.

"Peter's It!" Nibs shouted, sounding surprised at his luck.

Kate's feet kicked at the air. She wanted to play!

Just then, Peter swooped toward her. "Tag," he said, tapping Kate's head. He darted away, crying, "Can't catch me!"

"Oh yeah?" Kate shouted. Without another thought, she let go of Mia's hand and took off after him.

Kate's outstretched hand was inches from Peter's foot, when she heard a cry behind her. She turned and saw Mia paddling the air like a sinking swimmer. With a panicked look, Mia glanced down at the ground.

"No, don't!" Kate cried.

But it was too late. Mia started to fall.

Chapter 4

Tink was floating on the breeze when she saw Mia suddenly drop.

"Help her, Peter!" Tink cried out. But he was already diving through the air.

Peter's grace and speed were remarkable. He seemed to know it, too. He caught Mia just inches from the ground and flew an extra loop before setting her down.

The others landed around them.

"That was amazing!" Kate said.

"That was *scary*," Lainey said. "Mia, are you okay?"

Mia nodded. "I just need to sit for a second, that's all. Thanks for catching me," she said to Peter.

"It was nothing," Peter said with a shrug.

Tink thought Mia would be done with

flying for the day. She was surprised when Mia said, "I'm all right now. Should we go on?"

"Are you sure?" Tink asked. "You aren't afraid?"

"It's like riding a bike, right?" Mia said, glancing at Kate. "When you fall you just have to get right back on."

Tink could tell that Mia didn't want to miss whatever excitement lay ahead. She understood. She didn't want to miss it, either.

Peter seemed pleased. "Well, what are we waiting for? Let's go!"

They played Follow the Leader—or rather, Follow Peter, for he was always in the lead. When Peter banked left, the boys and girls followed like airplanes in formation. When Peter skimmed the trees, they did, too. Peter touched the pointed tip of each pine he passed, and one by one, the others did the same, surprising the birds and squirrels.

They flew across the Never forest—seven children and one fairy in a long, snaking line.

When they turned toward the coast, there was a headwind. Tink could fly fast, but she was much smaller than the boys and girls, so she tired quickly. She ended up riding on Peter's shoulder, as she'd done many times before.

It was lovely sitting there while Never Land rushed past beneath them. Tink wondered why she'd waited so long to visit her old friend.

When they came to an emerald-green cove, Peter began to spiral downward. The girls and boys followed.

They landed on a patch of white sand, surrounded by sea grass and palm trees. Nearby, a waterfall spilled over a cliff, pouring into the lagoon. To Tink it looked like any number of coves tucked into Never Land's shoreline. But the girls flew around, marveling over everything.

"Look at the waterfall!"

"Look at the water! Have you ever seen any so clear?"

"A dolphin!"

"Sea turtles!"

Peter stood by, grinning proudly, as if he'd invented it all himself.

After the long flight, the water was

inviting. The boys and girls jumped right in. Tink didn't swim. She couldn't fly if her wings got wet. But Peter knew one of the sea turtles—they'd met at a mermaid's party, he said—and he convinced it to carry Tink around on the water. Mia and Gabby picked grass from the shore and piled it onto the shell to make her more comfortable. Riding on her turtle ferry, Tink felt as grand as Queen Clarion herself.

On the beach, Nibs found a bubble of sea kelp the size of a baseball, and the boys and girls started a game of catch. Tink lazed on her sea turtle, sunning her wings, while the children splashed in the water, throwing the sea kelp bubble back and forth.

At some point, Tink noticed that Lainey had come to stand next to her in the shallows.

"Tired of playing?" Tink asked.

"I'm not such a good swimmer," Lainey admitted. "And no one was passing to me anyway."

Tink began to watch the game more closely. It seemed that every time Kate got the bubble, she threw it back to Peter. And every time Peter threw it to someone else, Kate intercepted.

"Over here, Kate!" Mia cried, as Kate caught another pass. But Kate sent the bubble sailing back to Peter.

Back and forth it went, the ball passing between Peter and Kate. Before long, Gabby came to stand next to Lainey and Tink. Then Cubby. Eventually, Mia and Nibs joined them, too.

"It's like she doesn't even see us," Mia said.

"Watch this, Peter!" Kate said, throwing the next pass from behind her back.

The throw went wide. The bubble sailed into the waterfall and disappeared.

"I'll get it!" Nibs cried. He seemed glad to have something to do.

Nibs flew behind the waterfall. He came back a minute later, excited. "There's nothing there!" he exclaimed.

"You mean you couldn't find the ball?" Kate asked.

"I mean there's nothing behind the waterfall," Nibs said. "It's just a big hole."

Of course, they all had to see for themselves. It was the kind of waterfall you could swim right under, so they did. Peter carried Tink cupped in his hands to keep her wings dry.

Behind the waterfall, they discovered a cave.

"Should we see where it goes?" Nibs asked.

Everyone looked to Peter. "We could," Peter said. "What do you think, Tink?"

Tink peered into the darkness. She thought that there were probably bats in there. Tink didn't want to have anything to do with bats.

But then Peter added, "You're the only one with a light, Tink. We'll get lost without you."

How could she refuse? "All right," she said. "Let's see where it goes."

chapter 5

Still at the mouth of the cave, Gabby hesitated. "I don't think I want to go in there," she said.

"Come on," Kate replied. "It'll be fun."

"But it's *spooky*," Gabby said.

"That's what makes it fun." Kate glanced into the cave. Their friends were disappearing into the darkness, unaware that Kate and Gabby had stopped.

"Wait!" Kate called. But the rush of

the waterfall drowned out her voice. Kate knew if they didn't stay close to Tink, they'd never find their way in the dark.

"Listen," she said, kneeling down to look Gabby in the eye. "If we don't go now, we'll miss all the fun. You don't want to get left behind, do you?"

"No, but—" Gabby started to say.

"Then again," Kate said, pretending to reconsider, "maybe it would be better if you stayed here and waited for us, since you're so little. Maybe just us bigger kids should go—"

"I'm not so little!" Gabby cried. "I can do anything Mia can do."

Kate smiled and took Gabby's hand. "Well, come on, then!"

After the bright sunshine outside, the

cave felt cool, like a cellar on a hot summer day. It smelled earthy and damp. As Kate's eyes adjusted to the darkness, she saw that the cave was bigger than she'd imagined. She could see Tink's light bobbing far ahead.

As they moved away from the entrance, Gabby's grip on Kate's hand tightened. "It's really dark—"

Her voice broke off as something furry brushed against them. Gabby screamed.

"Sorry," came Cubby's voice in the darkness. "I didn't see you. It's dark as a cave in here." He chuckled at his joke.

"I heard something growl," Gabby said.

"That was my stomach," Cubby admitted. "I get hungry when I'm nervous."

"Come on," Kate said, pulling them both forward. The cave was even spookier than she'd thought. She was relieved to see Tink flying toward them, their friends following behind. The group hurried into the dim circle of light cast by the fairy's glow.

"There you are!" Mia said when she saw Gabby. "I thought you were right behind me, but when I turned around, you were gone!"

"Can we go now?" Gabby said. "I don't like it in here."

"Wait," said Peter. "I think I saw something up there." He pointed toward the roof of the cave. "Tink, can you brighten your glow a little?"

"I'll try," said Tink. A second later, her glow flared.

Everyone gasped. They were standing in a great cavern. Giant formations that looked like cones dripped from the ceiling.

"Icicles!" Gabby cried.

"Not icicles," Lainey said. "They're stalactites. They're made of some kind of rock."

"Look how they sparkle!" Mia said.

They stood with their heads tipped back, as Tink flew around, lighting up the cave. There were dozens of them. Some were so big they dipped halfway to the ground.

"It's like a castle," Lainey said.

"A *magic* castle," Gabby agreed.

"See? I told you this would be cool," Kate said. She took a step forward and her foot struck something. Whatever it was clattered hollowly as it spun away.

"Tink, can you come here?" Kate called.

Tink flew over. Kate knelt down and saw that she'd kicked an empty glass bottle. "Where did this come from?" she wondered.

"There's another one here," Lainey said, nudging it with her foot. Tink flew closer to the ground. In her glow they caught glimpses of empty bottles, coils of rope, and what looked like some old clothes. They'd all been so busy looking at the ceiling that they hadn't noticed the cave was littered with objects.

"What is all this stuff?" Kate asked.

"I think we've found some pirates' hideout," Peter said.

"You mean *real* pirates?" Kate said,

looking at the junk with new interest. Their adventure was getting better by the minute!

As Tink flew slowly around, the kids picked up things they found on the cave floor. "Hey!" Lainey exclaimed. "A compass!"

"I found a biscuit!" declared Cubby.

"Don't eat that! It's dirty pirate food," Nibs said, knocking the bread from Cubby's hand. It spun away into the darkness.

"But it wasn't even nibbled." Cubby looked sadly at the spot where the biscuit had disappeared.

Kate poked through a pile of old wooden junk. *Maybe I'll find treasure!* she thought. *Or at least something cool, like a spyglass or a Jolly Roger flag.*

Mia came to stand next to her. "You don't think the pirates might come back while we're in here, do you?" she asked.

The cave fell quiet as everyone considered this.

Suddenly, from somewhere in the depths of the cave, they heard heavy footsteps. A rough voice growled, "And what's this? A bunch of scalawags come to plunder me loot?"

Kate went cold all over. She turned to see who had spoken. But at that moment the cave went black.

Where's Tink? she thought frantically. The fairy's light had disappeared, as if it had been snuffed out.

The footsteps came slowly closer, scraping on the cave floor. Kate tried to remember which way they'd come in. Was the exit blocked? Or could they escape somehow? Where was *Peter*?

Suddenly, Tink's glow flared again. On the wall of the cave they saw the terrible shadow of a pirate with his sword raised.

The scream was in Kate's throat, when suddenly the shadow began to dance. They heard a joyful laugh.

Peter came out from behind the stalagmite where he'd been hiding. He was wearing a pirate hat he'd found and holding his dagger. Tink fluttered in the air next to him, laughing, too. As she moved closer to Peter, his shadow grew. It was her light that had made his shadow seem so tall.

What a perfect prank! Kate thought.

All the kids were laughing now. "Good one, Peter," said Nibs. "You had us going!"

Encouraged, Peter growled in his pirate voice, "Arrgh! It's *Cap'n* Peter to the likes of you." He looked at Gabby and waggled his eyebrows. "So it's a duel you want? Raise yer weapon, ye lubber."

"Here." Nibs handed Gabby his sword. It had a dragon-shaped handle, and was so heavy that Gabby could barely lift it. But Peter played along, dancing around her and tapping at the sword with his dagger as if they were in a real duel. Gabby beamed as the others cheered them on.

Kate's hands itched to hold the sword, until finally she couldn't wait any longer. She stepped in and took the sword from the younger girl. "Here, Gabby," she said. "Let someone else have a try."

"Kate! I wasn't done!" Gabby said with a scowl.

Kate ignored her. She was waving the

sword, trying to get the hang of swinging it. Each time, Peter met her blade with his dagger.

"Will you teach me how to really swordfight?" she asked. "I always wanted to learn."

"Gladly," Peter said.

"I want to learn, too," Gabby said.

Kate laughed. "A pirate with fairy wings?" she added as Gabby's frown deepened. "What? I'm only teasing."

Peter soon had everyone laughing again. As they made their way back out of the cave, he taught them a pirate song. The cave echoed with the sound of their voices singing *"Yo ho ho."* They were having so much fun they forgot to pay attention to how long they'd been walking.

Mia was the first to notice. "Shouldn't

we be at the exit by now?" she asked.

Tink, who was leading, paused. "It does seem like we've gone too far," she said. "But look, there's light just up ahead."

"What's that sound?" Nibs asked.

Everyone went silent. Now they could clearly hear the *shush-shush* of waves on the shore.

"I don't remember hearing that on the way in," Lainey said.

They hurried toward the sunlight. But as they emerged from the cave, Kate knew something was wrong.

"Where's the waterfall?" she asked, looking around.

"I don't think this is the same cove as before," Lainey said. "This beach is covered with pebbles. The other beach had sand."

"It's not the same beach," Tink agreed, looking worried. "We took a wrong turn somewhere."

"Look!" Gabby yelled, pointing. Everyone turned.

A chill ran through Kate like a cloud crossing the sun.

A ship had entered the cove.

chapter 6

The ship looked very old. Its sails were tattered and its wood was gray. A wooden mermaid adorned the bow, her paint worn away by the sun and wind.

Onshore, the boys and girls watched warily. Kate knew by the Jolly Roger flying from its mast that it was a pirate ship.

"It's not a ship we've seen in Pirate Cove before," Nibs said.

"No, it's not," Peter agreed. "Let's wait and see who's aboard."

Several long minutes passed, but no one appeared on deck. No cannons fired. No lookout called from the crow's nest. There was no sign of life on the ship at all.

"I don't think there's *anyone* on board," Cubby said at last.

"It must be the Ghost Ship," Peter said.

"Ghost Ship?!" cried several voices at once. All eyes turned to Peter.

"You mean there are ghosts sailing it?" Lainey asked.

"No one knows for sure," Peter replied. "It moves about the sea without a captain or a crew. I've heard pirates tell stories about it. They say there's treasure in its hold—"

"Treasure?" Kate perked up.

Peter nodded. "So they say. But even the most fearsome pirates don't dare go on it. They say the ship is haunted and the souls on board are cursed."

Kate looked back out at the ship. The sun was just starting to set. In the fading light, the ship looked even spookier.

"Here's how we'll approach. Cubby, Mia, and Lainey, you'll fly in from starboard. Nibs, Kate, and—"

"Wait a second," Mia interrupted. "We're not really going onto that ship, are we?"

"Why not?" asked Peter.

"What about the ghosts?" asked Lainey.

"I'm not scared of them," said Peter. "I bet I can fly faster than any creaky old ghost."

"Well then, what about pirates?" Mia asked. "They might be hiding on board, just watching to see what we'll do."

"I think I can handle a pirate or two," Peter said, patting his dagger. Then understanding seemed to dawn on him. "Don't you *want* to go?"

For a moment no one said anything. Then Gabby shook her head.

"I don't want to go, either," said Lainey.

"Me either," Mia agreed.

Peter looked perplexed. "But it's going to be awfully fun!"

"I don't care," Mia said. "It's almost dark, and I'm hungry. It will be time for dinner soon."

At the word "dinner," Cubby's stomach complained loudly. "Peter," he said hesitantly. "Do you think maybe I should guide the girls back to Pixie Hollow? You know, in case of wild animals and whatnot."

"Right," Nibs agreed quickly. "Very dangerous. Maybe I should go, too."

Peter frowned at them. "Don't tell me you're both afraid of an old wooden ship?"

The boys looked embarrassed. "Pirates are one thing, Peter. But I don't want to meet a ghost," Cubby admitted.

"Well, off with you, then," he said gruffly. "No use hanging around."

Tink looked from the girls to Peter. Then she flew to his side, saying, "I'll go with you, Peter. You'll need someone to light the way."

Kate hesitated. She didn't want to leave. Not yet. The day with Peter had been thrilling, and she didn't want it to end. Not just to go home to another regular dinner at her boring old house.

Kate made a decision. "I'm going, too. I'm not afraid of ghosts," she added, though her heart was pounding.

"But what about our rule?" Mia whispered. The girls had a rule about Never

Land. One rule only—they went to the magic island together, and they returned home together. Always.

"What about it?" Kate said with a shrug. "You can wait for me in Pixie Hollow. I'll be back soon, and then we'll all go home together. I shouldn't have to miss out on an adventure just because *you* don't want to have one," she added.

The girls looked at each other uncertainly. "I don't know . . . ," Mia said.

"Are you coming, Kate?" Peter called. He and Tink were already starting out over the water.

"Go on," Kate told her friends. "I'll meet you back at the Home Tree."

And before they could say anything else, she rose into the air and chased after Peter.

"Nibs!" Peter called. Nibs turned back. "Give Kate your sword."

Nibs started to protest, but Peter cut him off. "You won't need it in Pixie Hollow."

Nibs reluctantly handed over the sword. He looked so sad to part with it that Kate almost gave it back. But he was already flying away with the others.

The clouds were stained red with sunset as Kate, Peter, and Tink set out across the cove. The water, which had been clear just moments before, looked murky now. The fish became slippery shadows.

A shiver ran through Kate. It might have been from the breeze that sprang up suddenly. Or the thrill of adventure. Or maybe it was a hint of something dangerous still to come.

Kate didn't have time to consider what had caused it. They'd reached the ship.

Chapter 7

As she hovered in the air, staring at the big, dark ship, Tink suddenly had second thoughts.

It wasn't because she was afraid. She'd been through plenty of pirate battles with Peter and the Lost Boys. She wasn't scared of a bit of danger.

What was bothering her was the thought of her mouse-powered well back in Pixie Hollow, and the promise she'd made to Silvermist and Fawn. She knew they'd be wondering where she was.

Tink had told herself she'd only go on one adventure that day. But one had become two, and two had become three. *That's how it always is with Peter,* she thought. The adventures came one after another, like beads on a string, until you couldn't even remember which one had started it all.

She wondered if she should have returned to Pixie Hollow with the other girls. She could still catch them if she flew fast.

As she hesitated, Peter flew over the side of the ship and landed lightly on the deck. Crouching down, he motioned for Tink and Kate to follow.

I can't turn back now, Tink thought. *Peter and Kate need me.* The sun was setting fast, and soon she'd be their only light.

And if Tink was being perfectly honest, she didn't *want* to go back to Pixie Hollow yet. Something exciting was bound to happen—and Tink wanted to see what it would be.

Just one more adventure, Tink told herself as she flew aboard.

Kate was right behind her. As she came over the side of the ship, Nibs's sword knocked against the wood. It fell onto the deck with a loud clatter.

Kate froze. Peter's dagger was out in a flash. They waited for a count of ten, but no one appeared.

"Come on," Peter whispered. They

crept across the deck like spies, crouching behind barrels and peering around masts. When they reached the stern, Peter finally lowered his weapon.

"I don't think there are any ghosts up here," he said. Tink could tell he was disappointed. He'd never battled a ghost, and Peter loved new experiences above all else.

"Maybe they're hiding," Kate said. "Maybe they're scared of *us.*"

Peter brightened at the thought. "Let's explore the hold!"

They found the stairs that led below deck. It was much darker there, so Tink led the way. In the hold they found several barrels. Most of them seemed to be empty.

"Phew!" Kate said, lifting the lid on one. "This smells like it used to have fish

in it." She replaced the lid and looked around. "Do you think that old pirate tale could be true? About there being treasure on the ship?"

"We could check the cabin," Peter suggested.

Tink flew in front again, brightening her glow to light the way. They found the captain's cabin at the other end of the ship. When they entered, Kate gasped. Thick silk rugs covered the floor. Velvet curtains hung on the tall, arched windows. In the center of the room was a heavy wooden table. Maps and charts were spread on top of it. Everything was faded and dusty, but the room had clearly once been grand.

"This is so *cool*!" Kate said. She went around the room, touching everything. "If I were a pirate, this is where I'd keep my treasure. Where do you suppose it's hidden?"

"I dunno," Peter said with a shrug. Treasure didn't interest him unless there was a good skirmish involved. He poked at one of the wine-colored curtains, as if hoping to find a ghost lurking behind it.

Tink didn't care about pirate treasure, either. She didn't have any use for jewels and gold coins in Pixie Hollow. But as she looked around, her eyes fell on a half-open drawer. She peered inside and gasped.

The drawer was full of trinkets—
buttons, clasps, knobs, and screws. To a
Clumsy, it was just a bunch of junk. But
to a tinkering fairy, it was treasure.

Tink held up one thing after another.
Her head was spinning with possibilities.
But which object should she take?

Why not take it all? she thought. *I can have Kate carry it in her pockets.*

"Kate, would you mind—" Tink started to say.

A scream cut her off. Tink spun around, but the cabin was empty. Kate and Peter were gone!

Then Tink heard Kate's voice. "Help me!" she cried.

Tink dropped the button she was holding. She began to fly toward Kate's voice. It was coming from somewhere below the cabin.

Just then, she heard a cry from the other side of the ship. "Help me! Kate, Tink, help!"

Peter!

Tink froze. In all the time she'd known

Peter, she'd never heard him yell for help.

"Help, Tink! Help!" Kate and Peter cried.

Tink fluttered back and forth in distress. Who should she go to? She started toward Peter, then changed her mind. Kate sounded closer. If she helped Kate first, maybe together they could save Peter.

But save him from what? Tink wondered. Her throat tightened with fear.

She had reached the steps that led down to the hold, when a figure came stumbling toward her. It was Kate! She was holding her side and grimacing.

No, not grimacing, Tink thought as Kate came closer. *Grinning.*

"Ha, ha!" Kate laughed. "Got you!"

"What's going on?" Tink stared at her

in confusion. Why was Kate laughing? Didn't she realize Peter was in trouble?

Then Peter flew up, and he was laughing, too. "We really fooled you, didn't we, Tink?" he said.

At last it sank in. It was only a joke. Tink's wings gave out, and she had to sit down.

"It was funny, wasn't it?" Peter said, still chuckling.

Tink gave him a half smile. She remembered now why she had stopped hanging around with Peter. It wasn't because she no longer cared for him. He was the same charming, childish, marvelous, exasperating Peter he'd always been, and Tink adored him. But there were things she liked even better than his adventures.

When her wings felt steady enough to fly again, Tink rose into the air.

"Where are you going?" Kate asked. She sounded surprised.

"Home," said Tink. Then she set off toward Pixie Hollow, where her tinkering workshop was waiting, and where, she knew, her fairy friends would be waiting, too.

chapter 8

"I wonder what got into her?" Peter said as Tink flew away.

"Beats me," Kate said. But as she watched Tink's light growing smaller, she felt a pang of regret. When she'd whispered the prank in Peter's ear, it had seemed funny. Kate thought they'd give Tink a little scare and they'd all have a good laugh over it, like they had when Peter and Tink tricked them in the cave.

But when she'd seen how truly frightened Tink looked, the joke didn't seem so funny after all.

Peter seemed to have already forgotten about Tink. He was playing with the big wooden ship's wheel. He hovered in the air above it, pretending to steer it with his feet.

Kate watched him. "I guess there isn't any treasure aboard this ship after all," she said with a sigh.

Peter shrugged. "Who cares about gold and jewels? This *ship* is our treasure. Let's take her somewhere."

"But I don't know how to sail," Kate said.

"Aw, there's nothing to it," Peter told her. "You just shout 'Anchors aweigh!' and 'Head to the wind!' and off you go!"

Kate laughed. "Where would we go?"

"Anywhere," said Peter. He was hopping up and down with excitement. "We can sail all the way to the mainland if we want!"

Kate imagined sailing all the way home in an ancient pirate ship. What a blast that would be! Of course, there was no ocean near her city, but that didn't matter. In her imagination, she and Peter sailed the ship through the air, right up to her front door. She pictured the astonished expressions on her parents' and neighbors' faces as she waved to them from the bow. Kate giggled.

Peter was letting out the sails. "Are you really going sailing now?" Kate asked.

"Why not?" said Peter.

"But it's nighttime!"

"We'll set our course by the stars and sail by the light of the moon," Peter replied. "And the wind's an old friend of mine. He'll keep us straight and true."

Was he telling stories again? It was always so hard to tell. But Kate wanted to believe him. Sailing all the way home—it would be the biggest adventure yet!

"But, oh—" Kate thought of Mia, Lainey, and Gabby waiting for her in Pixie Hollow. She couldn't leave without them.

"I'd want my friends to come, too," she told Peter. "And what about Cubby and Nibs and the other boys?"

Peter thought about it, then nodded. "It *would* be better for games of hide-and-seek at sea. We'll round up the crew and sail

at dawn. But I'll sleep on my ship tonight like any good captain."

Kate agreed to stay with Peter. She didn't like the thought of sleeping on that spooky ship. But she decided that if Peter wasn't scared, then she wouldn't be, either. Besides, flying all the way back to Pixie Hollow alone didn't seem much better.

The last bit of sun was gone. The pale twilight was darkening into inky night. To Kate's relief, Peter declared there was no point in exploring the ship any more. Without Tink's light, they couldn't see a thing.

Instead, they sat on deck and watched the stars come out. Peter pointed out constellations—the Sparrow, the Guppy, the Greater Foot and the Lesser Foot, Starkey's Hat. Kate had the feeling that he was making them up as he went along. But it was pleasant sitting there, watching his finger trail through the sky. She could almost see the shapes in the stars.

They talked about their adventures. Kate told him about Cloud, the mist horse she'd tamed and ridden across Never Land. She told him about winning goals she'd scored in soccer and about the

time she'd broken her arm trying to slide down the banister at her grandmother's house. For every story Kate had, though, Peter seemed to have a hundred. He'd flown with eagles and visited stars and played tricks on elves and battled dozens of pirates. But when she pressed him, he was always fuzzy about the details.

"What was the name of the pirate you defeated on Skull Rock?" she asked.

"Him? Oh, that was Barbecue," Peter replied.

"I thought you said Barbecue met his end at sea," Kate said.

"Did I?" said Peter. "Well then, it must have been Bonnet. Yes, I'm sure it was Bonnet."

"It sounds exciting," said Kate, wrapping her arms around her knees.

"It was," said Peter.

Kate leaned against Peter's shoulder. Her eyelids felt heavy. Before she knew it, she'd fallen asleep.

She woke sometime later. She was lying curled up on deck. The arm that had been touching Peter's shoulder was cold.

Kate sat up. "Peter?" she said, looking around.

There was no reply. Kate got to her feet, calling louder. "Peter?"

The only sound was the slap of waves against the hull. The shore looked far away. With a start, Kate realized the ship was floating out to sea. And Peter was gone.

chapter 9

At first, Kate thought it was another one of Peter's jokes. She expected him to pop out from behind the mast at any moment, or spring up from a coil of rope, shouting "Boo!"

But minutes passed, and Peter didn't appear. Kate slumped against the ship's helm, shivering. Before, the ship had been merely spooky. But now, in the moonlight, the shadows seemed menacing. Her ears were alert to every sound. Was that the wind in the rigging? Or was it a ghostly voice?

At one point Kate was certain she heard a splash. Her heart nearly leaped into her throat.

It was a fish jumping. That's all, she told herself.

But what if it wasn't? What if the ship wasn't really abandoned? What if it belonged to pirates who had gone ashore to bury their treasure and were on their way back this very minute? Was it the splash of their rowboat oars she'd heard?

Kate waited, frozen with dread. She was still holding Nibs's sword, though she knew it wouldn't be much use. After all, what could *she* do with a sword against a real pirate?

Several times she considered flying

away. But the thought that Peter might need her help kept her there. What had happened to him? she wondered. Was he lost somewhere in the ship's hold? Had he fallen and hit his head? Or had a ghost gotten him after all?

The moon rose. The night grew cooler. Kate's eyes kept playing tricks on her. When she spied a shape slipping over the side of the ship, she wasn't sure if it was real.

Then the figure stepped into the moonlight, and she saw that it was Peter. He was as wet as a seal, and grinning.

"Where have you been?" Kate asked. Her voice came out in a croak.

"Just now? I was talking to a mermaid," Peter replied. "I was telling her the funniest story."

"But you've been gone for ages!" Kate said.

"Have I?" Peter asked with genuine surprise. "It didn't seem long at all."

"I've been here all by myself. I was waiting for you!" Kate stopped just short of telling him how scared she'd been.

"I'm sorry. I guess I forgot," Peter

replied. "Why didn't you just fly off and do something fun until I got back?"

Kate stared at him. It dawned on her that he didn't understand why she was upset. Possibly he *couldn't* understand. In the short time she'd known him, she'd never seen him afraid of anything.

"I was worried about you," she said.

"What for?" Peter asked. "Listen, I have an idea. Let's wake up the Lost Boys and the other girls and set sail now. The moon's nice and bright tonight."

Kate stood up stiffly. "I don't think I want to go anymore," she said. Sailing to the mainland with Peter didn't seem quite like the adventure it had before. "I think I just want to go home."

Peter's brow wrinkled. "Why would you do that?" he asked.

He really doesn't understand, Kate thought. *He only cares about playing games and having fun.* Peter was the most exciting person she'd ever met. But for once, Kate was tired of excitement.

She climbed up on the side of the ship. "I'll see you around Never Land," she said.

"You're really leaving?" Peter looked disappointed. But a second later, he brightened. "Maybe the next time you see me, I'll have sailed this ship around the world. What an awfully big adventure that would be!"

He probably will, too, Kate thought. Peter seemed able to do just about anything. She smiled. "I can't wait to hear about it," she said.

Then she rose into the air and set out for Pixie Hollow.

When Kate reached the shore, she looked back toward the ship. Peter was still at the wheel, shouting things like "All hands on deck!" and "Smartly, now!" He looked as if he was having the time of his life.

chapter 10

Back in Pixie Hollow, the Home Tree was dark and quiet. But a light blazed in the window of Tinker Bell's workshop.

Inside, Tink was busy searching the shelves where she kept her found things. Sometimes Clumsy objects washed up on the shore of Never Land. Tink polished them to use them in her inventions.

"This hinge will work," she said to herself. "And I can use this scrap of metal. Now, where is that four-hole button?"

When Tink had gotten back to Pixie Hollow that evening, she'd found her fairy friends waiting for her—Silvermist and Fawn, as well as Rosetta, Prilla, and Iridessa. Even the fast-flying fairy Vidia had been there, though she'd pretended she was just passing by. They greeted Tink with tears and hugs, as if she'd returned from a long journey. Tink had scoffed at all the fuss. But secretly she was pleased.

It was late now. All her friends were asleep in their rooms high in the Home Tree's branches. But Tink didn't feel sleepy. Her mind was whirling with plans.

The adventures that day had given her ideas for several new inventions— like a mechanical turtle boat, with four paddles that moved like flippers, and a shadow lantern that spun and projected spooky shadow plays on the wall. And of course, Tink still wanted to fix her mouse-powered well. She had an idea for how a button could work as an emergency brake.

She had just found the button beneath a pile of polishing rags when she heard a soft *thump-thump* on her door.

That's not a fairy's knock, Tink thought. She went to the window and peeped out. "Who's there?"

"It's me, Kate," came the girl's voice. "I saw your light on."

Tink was surprised. It was a long way back to Pixie Hollow in the dark. "Is Peter with you?" she asked.

"No," said Kate. "Will you come outside? It's hard to talk through the door."

Tink sighed. Was this another prank? "I'm very busy," she said. "I have a lot of tinkering to do—"

"Just for a minute," Kate pleaded.

"Oh, all right." Tink opened the door.

Kate was crouched at the roots of the Home Tree, just outside Tink's workshop. Her red hair was windblown from the long flight back.

"Well, what is it?" Tink asked.

"I'm sorry," Kate said. "It was my idea to play that trick on you. It wasn't very nice."

"It wasn't," Tink agreed. Was this what Kate had come back for? she wondered. An apology could have waited until morning.

"You must be really mad at me," Kate went on. "I spoiled the whole adventure for you."

Tink shook her head. "You didn't spoil it. I could have stayed if I'd wanted."

"Why didn't you?" Kate asked.

"There were other things I wanted to do," Tink replied. "Adventures aren't everything, you know."

"Peter thinks they are," said Kate.

Tink smiled. "Well, Peter is Peter. If he

was a fairy, he'd have a talent for adventures." She looked at Kate curiously. "Why did *you* come back?"

"I don't know." Kate sighed. "We were going to sail the ship all the way to the mainland. It would have been the most exciting thing I'd ever done, and part of me still wishes I had gone. But another part of me just wanted to go home. Isn't that weird?"

"Not really," said Tink.

Kate stood up. "I was supposed to meet Mia and Lainey and Gabby back here hours ago. They probably went home without me. I guess I don't blame them," she added.

"They're still here," Tink told her. "They're waiting for you in the willow tree room." The willow tree was where the girls had slept the first time they spent the night in Pixie Hollow.

Just then, they heard voices coming toward them, speaking in whispers.

"It's so dark out! I *told* you guys we should have left earlier."

"It was dark then, too!"

"I wish we had a flashlight."

"How are we going to find the right cove at night?"

"Maybe we should wake one of the fairies and ask her to come with us."

"Ow! Gabby, you stepped on my foot!"

"You guys!" Kate cried, running to her friends. A second later, the girls were wrapped in a four-way hug.

"We were just coming to find you," Lainey told her.

"None of us could sleep," Gabby explained. "We kept thinking about you on that scary ship."

"We shouldn't have left you behind," Mia said. "Are you really mad at us?"

"No way!" Kate said. "I thought *you'd* be mad at me for staying there without you."

"Well then, it's settled," said Mia. "The next time we come across a big, spooky ghost ship, we all stick together."

"If there is a next time," Lainey added.

"What do you mean?" Kate said with a laugh. "There's always a next time in Never Land."

The other girls didn't seem to notice Tink. She fluttered into her workshop. As she went back to the plans for her latest invention, she could still hear them talking.

"So what happened on the ship?" Mia was asking Kate. "Did you see a ghost?"

"Did you find the treasure?" Gabby asked.

"Not exactly," Kate said, then quickly added, "But it was still pretty exciting." She put an arm around Mia's shoulders and another around Lainey's. "Let's go home. I'll tell you all about it on the way."

Read this Sneak peek of Before the Bell, the Next Never Girls adventure!

Gabby knew most of the sparrow men in Pixie Hollow, but she'd never seen this one before. He wore an oak-leaf vest with many patches. His hair stuck out every which way from beneath his stocking cap. And his shoes were so full of holes that Gabby could see his toes peeping out.

"Spinner's back!" Beck cried, jumping to her feet.

The sparrow man fluttered down, and the fairies surrounded him, welcoming him with smiles and hugs. Spinner returned their happy greetings, but his eyes kept traveling back to Gabby. "I hope you don't mind my saying so," he said at last, "but you're the biggest fairy I've ever seen."

"What? Oh!" Gabby laughed. He'd noticed her dress-up fairy wings! "I'm not a fairy. I'm a girl."

"She's an honorary fairy," said Iridessa.

Spinner looked impressed. "Well, I'll be jammed and jellied. You're the first honorary fairy I've met. What's your name?"

When Gabby told him, he chuckled. "I'm a bit 'gabby' myself. You and I will get along just fine."

"You've been gone a long time," Iridessa said to Spinner.

The sparrow man nodded. "A dozen moons at least. And I have as many stories to tell."

"Spinner is a story-talent fairy," Silvermist explained to Gabby. "He travels all over collecting tales. Then he brings them back to Pixie Hollow."

A story talent! Gabby had never met a story talent before. She squatted down to get a better look. "What kind of tales?" she asked him.

Spinner's eyes lit up. "Would you like to hear one?"

"Yes! Tell us a story!" the fairies all exclaimed. They sat down to listen. Gabby sat, too, wrapping her arms around her knees.

"It all started one afternoon when I was in the forest eating Never Berries," Spinner began. "Now, as anyone who's ever had a Never Berry knows, there's nothing more delicious. Why, I'd say they taste just like a summer sunrise. . . ."

As he spoke, a strange thing happened. Gabby's mouth filled with a fresh, juicy taste, a flavor as sweet as strawberries and as bright as lemons. It was as if she were inside Spinner's story, eating berries right along with him.

"Before long I noticed a bird gobbling up the berries, too," Spinner went on. "He had an ivory beak and silver feathers. I knew he wasn't from Never Land."

Gabby could see the bird as clearly as if it were sitting next to her. Its white beak was stained with pink berry juice. Its feathers gleamed in the sunlight.

"I said to the bird, 'These berries are the finest food you'll ever taste.' But the bird puffed himself up and said, 'I've had better. Where I'm from, there's a cake as sweet and light as a dream. It's made from stardust and baked in moonlight.' Well, I knew I had to try that cake. So when the bird left, I hitched a ride. . . ."

Spinner kept talking, but Gabby no longer heard the words. She was suddenly in the story, riding on the silver bird's back.